BLACK BLIZZARD

KRISTIN F. JOHNSON

MINNEAPOLIS

Darby Creek
A division of Lerner Publishing Group, Inc.
241 First Avenue North
Minneapolis, MN 55401 USA

For reading levels and more information, look up this title at www.lernerbooks.com.

Front cover: © iStockphoto.com/Scott Cramer; © iStockphoto.com/carton_king,(dust swirls); © Andrey Armyagov/Shutterstock.com, (school bus).

Images in this book used with the permission of: © iStockphoto.com/Scott Cramer; © iStockphoto.com/carton_king,(dust swirls); © Andrey Armyagov/Shutterstock.com, (school bus); © iStockphoto.com/Marina Mariya (swirl).

Main body text set in Janson Text LT Std 12/17.5.
Typeface provided by Adobe Systems.

Library of Congress Cataloging-in-Publication Data

Names: Johnson, Kristin F., 1968- author.
Title: Black blizzard / Kristin F. Johnson.
Description: Minneapolis : Darby Creek, [2017] | Series: Day of disaster | Summary: "A team's school bus breaks down in the middle of the desert after a disappointing loss at the State Championships, and a gathering dust storm threatens to turn their bus into a death trap. It will take some quick thinking to get through this!"— Provided by publisher.
Identifiers: LCCN 2016017982 (print) | LCCN 2016034213 (ebook) | ISBN 9781512427745 (lb : alk. paper) | ISBN 9781512430936 (pb : alk. paper) | ISBN 9781512427813 (eb pdf)
Subjects: | CYAC: Dust storms—Fiction. | Survival—Fiction. | Arizona—Fiction.
Classification: LCC PZ7.1.J624 Bl 2017 (print) | LCC PZ7.1.J624 (ebook) | DDC [Fic]—dc23

LC record available at https://lccn.loc.gov/2016017982

Manufactured in the United States of America
1-41499-23360-5/16/2016

For Alisa

1

The day of the disaster, Tyler Manning couldn't believe he had screwed up so badly. He leaned over and rested his forehead against the seatback. He clutched his cell phone in his hand, trying to focus on the maze game he'd downloaded the week before. Usually he could finish a level within a few minutes, but today he just wasn't thinking clearly.

The school bus lurched, jolting Tyler backward and forward so his head smacked on the seat in front of him. He dropped his phone. It skidded up the floor, crashing into the pair of feet in front of him.

"Hey!" Sha'relle snapped, pulling off her headphones. Sha'relle's music was playing so loud that even in the seat behind her Tyler could hear it was Beyoncé.

"Yeah, watch it," her seatmate Daniela said, glaring back at Tyler.

"Sorry." Tyler rubbed his forehead where he had smacked it on the seat. He felt around on the floor until he found his phone.

His phone had lost service once the bus had gotten far enough into the middle of nowhere. Tyler wished he had some music saved on his phone since he could no longer connect to his streaming app, but normally he wouldn't have needed it because he and Ethan would have been talking the whole way home. That's what they did for the past speech-team events they'd gone to this year.

Instead Ethan sat two rows back with L.J., who was in the spot Tyler had occupied on the way to the state tournament—right across the aisle from where Julia Evans sat. Since they left the tournament, Ethan had acted as if he didn't even know Tyler.

The panels of the bus's front door were rattling. The way they rattled, one side had to be loose. Tyler wondered if the school district saved the rundown buses for these Saturday speech tournaments.

The bus rumbled down Interstate 10 through the Arizona desert. The trip back to Phoenix was a torturous hour and forty-five minutes. Normally, that didn't seem far, but today it felt like the longest ride ever—and they were only halfway there. Through his window, Tyler saw endless acacia trees, buckthorn, desert willow trees, and deer grass. On the way to Tucson, Tyler's teammates had been all fired up, goofing around and practicing speeches for their events. But no one had that energy anymore after losing at State.

With a sudden popping sound, the bus sputtered and lurched and slowed down. The driver struggled to pull over to the side of the road.

"Why are we stopping?" Sha'relle asked, kneeling up on her seat.

"Probably ran out of gas," José said. Other students leaned up in their seats to get a better look. The noise inside the bus grew as they began chattering about what they thought the problem might be.

Tyler spotted smoke escaping from under the front of the bus.

The bus driver reached down from his seat, pulled a latch, and popped the hood. He whispered something to their speech-team coach, Mr. Dwyer, who then stood in the aisle and faced the team. The loose door shuddered as the driver opened it.

"Everyone calm down. The driver needs to check something under the hood. We should be back on the road shortly." Mr. Dwyer adjusted his baseball cap and scratched his beard. Tyler frowned. Their coach usually wasn't a fidgety guy. He hadn't even seemed this anxious at their tournament earlier that day. Something seemed seriously wrong.

"We can't get stuck here. I have plans tonight," Sha'relle said.

"Yeah," Daniela piped up. "Me, too."

"Take your seats, everyone. Just give us five minutes while we figure this out," Mr. Dwyer replied.

Sha'relle finally sat down.

Mr. Dwyer swung around the front handrail and met the bus driver outside. He continued his beard-scratching and cap-adjusting as he spoke with the driver and pointed under the hood. The driver waved his arms and wiped sweat off his brow. *That dude sweats a lot,* Tyler thought to himself.

A wind picked up and blew Mr. Dwyer's baseball cap right off his head and he ran after it. Whenever he got close to the cap, it lifted off the ground and traveled another five feet away. José and Kevin pointed from their seats and laughed. It did look like a comedy skit, but it was weird to see their coach so out of it. He was usually a pretty calm, thought-out guy—it was one of the reasons Mr. Dwyer was one of Tyler's favorite teachers.

Mr. Dwyer crouched down and finally caught his hat.

Smoke continued rolling out from under the hood of the bus—that couldn't be good. The wind blew the smoke sideways. Tyler watched as the bus driver stepped away from the hood and slammed it closed. The driver tore off his own hat and threw it on the ground in a fit. Almost immediately, his eyes looked over to the bus. By the way the man's gaze drifted along a number of the windows, Tyler figured he wasn't the only student who'd seen the driver do that. Several people were now leaning against the windows to see what was happening outside. The driver sheepishly glanced around and picked up his hat.

"Yep, we're stalled," Sha'relle said.

"Not just stalled," Kevin corrected. "This bus has broken down."

Tyler looked down the road in both directions. They were in the middle of the desert, alone on the side of the road, with no towns in sight.

"Aw, man!" said L.J. "I wanted to be home to watch the Sun Devils. ASU is in the playoffs!"

Mr. Dwyer climbed back onto the bus. A

moment later, the bus driver clambered up the steps and whispered something to Mr. Dwyer again.

"All right, everyone, listen up," Mr. Dwyer said. "The bus has broken down."

Groans.

"Told you," Kevin said to anyone who would listen.

"I know. I'm not happy about it either," Mr. Dwyer said. "The bus driver is calling for a replacement. Just sit tight until it arrives. Shouldn't be long."

The bus driver picked up the two-way radio hand piece, which crackled with static. "Hello? Hello?" He looked up for a second to see if anyone was watching. Pretty much everyone was watching.

What would Dad do? Tyler wondered. His dad was horrible with cars. He would probably call Triple-A. Tyler checked his phone again— still no bars.

Tyler looked out the window. *That's just great*, he thought. *Let's make this horrible ride home even longer.* A clump of tumbleweed rolled by, much faster than ones he had seen earlier. Beyond the tumbleweed, clouds formed as if nighttime was approaching, but it was only mid-afternoon. The surrounding sky grew darker. Tyler studied the clouds again. They looked like a haze of gathering dust.

2

The screwup at the speech tournament was one of those moments Tyler often had nightmares about, but the nightmares hadn't come true until today.

The worst part was that Tyler's event came at the end of the day. By then, his teammates had all finished their competitions and knew their team's score and ranking, so everyone was watching Tyler. His storytelling performance would affect the overall placement of the team and everyone was counting on him to nail it.

And then he froze.

In the moments before he took the stage, he should have been turning over the first few lines in his head so he could ensure a strong opening delivery, but instead all he could think about was how L.J. had sidled up to Julia all day and kept chatting with her and touching her arm.

When it came time for Tyler to begin, he'd walked up to the podium on stage, squinting into the bright spotlight . . . and his mind went blank.

Tyler glanced around the auditorium. He'd completely forgotten the first sentence. He stood in silence for what felt like an hour before he finally stammered something. Once he got back on track, it was too late. The opening was worth a huge chunk of points, and he had blown it. And now he just had to keep going, because all eyes were on him. He felt himself sweating. The next time he spoke, the microphone made that horrible sound.

SCREEEEECH!

Feedback.

The audience members covered their ears. The feedback problem wasn't Tyler's fault, but it probably added to his poor score because it threw him off even more.

After that disaster, instead of Tyler getting the usual congratulatory pats on the back, he felt the stares of disappointed teammates.

Since he had blanked on his storytelling piece, his team lost nearly all the points for that category and the team wound up losing the tournament. The Kennedy High School Speech Team made it to State because of their best season in three years, but now they had to go home defeated.

It was the team's worst loss since Tyler could remember. His dad had been impressed Tyler had chosen speech club because, as he liked to joke, most adults feared public speaking more than death. Tyler's dad wouldn't be so impressed to know Tyler had lost the competition for the team. Maybe he wouldn't tell his dad what happened.

But the real reason Tyler joined speech had nothing to do with pleasing his dad. He'd been interested mainly because it was co-ed and specifically because Julia Evans was on the team. Tyler had had a crush on her since ninth grade. She was pretty and smart—a win-win. She was also good at video games, which was cool. Tyler wanted to ask her to their school's Spring Fling dance, but if he asked her right now—right after his big flop—she was sure to say no. The dance was a month away. If Tyler didn't ask her soon, someone else might— someone like Lucas Jones.

The worst part of today's defeat was that Lucas Jones, called L.J. for short, had nailed his category, scoring the highest points for the team. And it was obvious to everyone on the team that L.J. was into Julia. Julia was a sophomore like Tyler, but L.J. was a junior, and it seemed like he could date anyone he wanted. Why did he have to pick the one girl Tyler was interested in?

Tyler's mouth grew dry. That wasn't unusual lately, since pretty much *everything* in Arizona was dry. His dad said the drought this year was worrisome. His dad sold orange fencing to farmers, so he talked to a lot of them, and drought was a favorite conversation topic.

When droughts happened, the state was ripe for other problems. In school, Tyler's class studied the Dust Bowl of the 1930s, which was known as the worst dry spell in American history. The Dust Bowl had caused huge dust storms and crop failures in nearby states like New Mexico. Tyler could remember Ethan's competitive speech on the Dust Bowl from the last tournament.

The whole bus was quiet and tense except for Kevin and José, who kept telling stupid jokes in the back row. Mr. Dwyer always told a joke at the beginning of physics class, but his jokes weren't as dirty as the ones Kevin and José were telling.

There were twenty kids on the speech team, and they all came along for the State Tournament. The bus had more than twenty seats, so some people could have a bench to themselves if they wanted one. Tyler was one of those sitting alone.

It was true that Tyler wanted to be alone, but he hated to think that no one wanted to sit with him because of his screwup. *Be careful what you wish for*, people always say. That empty space on the bench seat beside him crushed Tyler. He gave up on the maze game on his phone and couldn't help himself from glancing over his shoulder to look two rows behind him.

Julia was quietly reading a book, ignoring the noise from the others on the bus. He couldn't see the cover but she'd been reading it the entire bus ride on the way to the tournament as well, so Tyler figured she had to be enjoying the book. He turned to face forward, wondering if it would be weird to ask her what she was reading. She had good taste in video games, so she had to like some good books too. Just as he was working up the nerve to turn back to her, L.J. also seemed to notice what she was doing.

"Hey, Julia." L.J.'s voice carried up the aisle to Tyler. "What are you reading?"

"Have you heard about this new sci-fi trilogy that takes place on Mars? This is the first book in the series," Julia said. "I just started it."

Tyler had to force himself not to turn around and glare at L.J. So much for his own interest in her book. If he asked now he would look like he was just copying L.J., even if Tyler actually was curious about what she thought of the book. He would have to think of another conversation starter.

"Cool. You'll have to tell me how it is," L.J. said.

Tyler couldn't resist the urge to see how Julia reacted to this. He peered over his shoulder in time to see L.J. nudge Julia's arm, which made Tyler want to jump out of his seat and block their eye contact across the aisle.

Ethan, sitting next to L.J., looked up at Tyler. Tyler straightened in his seat, but then Ethan turned back to L.J. and said something Tyler couldn't hear. L.J. laughed and nodded. Jerks. The speech team had always been like a second family to Tyler. How could family turn on you like that, after one lousy mistake?

Tyler had told Ethan of his plan to ask Julia to the Spring Fling. He prayed Ethan wouldn't tell anyone, especially L.J. The last thing Tyler needed was competition from someone who was older, someone who was a better speaker, someone who had his own car.

L.J. was always bragging about how his dad had gotten him a sweet Honda coupe for his sixteenth birthday last year. Tyler's dad didn't think Tyler needed his own car with only two of them in the house. But Tyler planned to take his driver's test as soon as he turned sixteen next month and he'd started saving as much money as he could so he could buy his own car anyway. L.J. hadn't needed to do anything to get his car. He just had everything handed to him, but Tyler had to work for everything. His dad's philosophy was that *you appreciate things more if you have to earn them.*

Ethan and L.J. laughed at something again. They weren't talking about him, Tyler reminded himself. Or were they?

Julia was absorbed in her book again. Any opportunity to start a conversation with her seemed to be gone at this point. Tyler had hoped being in speech club would give him more confidence when talking to girls. Now Tyler felt he was back to square one.

He wanted to tune out everyone, but sounds seemed magnified today. His ears popped, which sometimes happened when a thunderstorm was coming, but the air had been so dry he couldn't imagine they would get any rain.

He was sweating more than usual, either from the stress of losing the tournament or from the heat of the day. He kept his arms down, trying to hide the stains on his shirt. All he wanted to do after letting everyone down was to crawl into his bed at home and hide his head under the pillow.

Sitting there waiting for the replacement bus was excruciating. The dark leather seats heated in the sun.

"Does anyone else feel like they're baking on this bus?" Sha'relle asked, wiping a hand across her forehead.

Tyler shook out his shirt to cool down. Outside, he saw another tumbleweed roll by.

Sha'relle and Daniela fanned themselves with their speech notes.

"Why are those cacti bending like that?" Julia asked. Tyler glanced back at her and saw that she was pointing out her window. He looked where she pointed.

The group of cacti was bent sideways at a forty-five degree angle. The wind around them was picking up.

3

Tyler looked at his watch. 4:13 p.m.

"Should the sky be this dark already?" he asked.

"I'm going to say no," Julia answered him. She turned in her seat and looked at the sky all around them. Toward Phoenix, their destination, the sky was blue and clear. But the sky toward Tucson was gray, almost black. The sun was low on the horizon.

"Were we supposed to get a storm?" Julia asked.

"I don't think so," Tyler said. It hadn't rained all spring, thanks to the drought Tyler's dad had kept going on about. His dad said it would be the worst drought they'd seen in years.

"Rainstorms usually don't look like that," Ethan pointed out.

A prairie dog ran up to the bus. The little creature stood on his haunches with his eyes darting back and forth as if he had gulped down too many energy drinks. Then he scurried off and ducked into a nearby hole. Tyler would have mistaken the hole for a snake hole if he hadn't just seen the prairie dog dive into it.

Tyler and Julia saw the prairie dog at the same time and caught each other's eyes. Tyler was no animal expert but he figured that if even the animals were looking for cover, some serious weather must be coming their way.

Behind them, what looked like a wall of brown clouds moved closer. One by one, kids began to head off the bus to see what was going on.

"Hey, stay on the bus. Guys—" Mr. Dwyer stood as the students rushed past him. He sighed, lifting his hat to wipe at his forehead before following them out of the bus.

"Dust storm," José said.

"Awesome!" Kevin yelled.

When Tyler stepped off the bus, the hot air caught his breath. He loosened his tie. Good thing he'd brought his inhaler. He never went anywhere without it. Not being able to breathe was the scariest feeling ever. Out in the desert, he felt like he was breathing while sitting in a sauna, except this air wasn't just dry. It was full of dust particles that coated his mouth. Tyler wore braces and the thought of dust and dirt on his braces made him wince.

Pretty soon, everyone had exited the bus. The whole team stood outside and pointed at the approaching clouds.

"I've never seen anything like that," Sha'relle murmured.

"It's heading this way," Kevin said.

The driver came out to stand near Tyler. As he stared at the brewing clouds, his mouth gaped open. He clutched his hat, crushing it in his grip. "Sweet mother of mercy."

The driver hopped back on the bus and into his seat. He revved the engine, pressing on the gas a few times. The engine groaned as if it was in pain. The driver turned the key and tried again. The gears were grinding. "Come on! Come on!" He pumped the gas several more times, which probably just flooded the engine.

Nothing.

He hit the steering wheel with his hands and gave up. That bus was not going anywhere.

Tyler looked down the road. No towns in sight—no gas stations—no cars.

"We could outrun it," L.J. suggested. "Dust storms don't travel very fast, do they?"

"About twenty-five miles per hour," said Ethan, probably remembering that information from his presentation.

L.J. *was* a fast runner, but who would want to run with that dust cloud chasing him?

"No," Mr. Dwyer said. "We're staying with the bus." He looked at L.J. "All of us."

"But there's probably a town just a few miles away," L.J. argued.

"Did you bring running shoes?"

L.J. looked down at himself. He wore black dress shoes with his dress pants and suit jacket. "I can run in these."

"Well, you aren't going to," Mr. Dwyer said. "This isn't a debate."

"Yeah," Tyler said. "Quit arguing."

"Well, what do you suggest, genius?" L.J. said. When Tyler said nothing, he added, "Then again, maybe we shouldn't be asking you for advice. It hasn't exactly been your day, has it?"

Tyler clenched his fists, then looked down. The ground had shifted into mini-sand dunes. He'd never get over being the reason the team lost at State. What if this embarrassing loss followed him around for the rest of high school?

"Lay off him, L.J." Ethan elbowed L.J. Tyler was surprised but also relieved that Ethan was coming to his defense.

The dust storm kept moving but approached slowly, the way water comes to a boil.

Earlier that year, a firefighter had come to Kennedy High School and given the annual safety talk in the auditorium. Dust storms were becoming more common, he'd said, so they were getting more attention as a result. The firefighter taught them the motto from the National Weather Service for what to do in case of a dust storm: *Pull aside. Stay alive!*

Well, Tyler thought, they were already pulled aside because the bus broke down. So they were following that direction. Now they needed to know what to do if the storm actually reached them—and it looked like it would very soon.

"How much time do you think we have?" Tyler asked.

Mr. Dwyer pulled out his phone, glancing at the clock on the lock screen. "Maybe twenty or thirty minutes. The dust cloud's moving pretty steady." He fiddled with it for a bit before sighing and looking up at the students.

"Does anyone have service? We should try to make a call."

Though he'd just looked at it minutes ago, Tyler pulled his own phone out of his pocket along with the other students to check. A few of them even held their phones up in the air as if that would help them get service. They were far enough from the nearest cell tower that apparently none of their phones could get a strong enough signal.

"If all that dust gets in the air, how will anyone be able to breathe?" Daniela asked suddenly.

"That's the point," L.J. said. "We *won't* be able to breathe. We need to be inside a building. Which is why I think we should start running."

"No one is running anywhere," Mr. Dwyer ordered.

"We don't have air tanks. We can't hold our breath. How are we going to last in the middle of that dust cloud?" L.J. was getting more agitated.

"We'll seal the bus the best we can," Mr. Dwyer said.

Ethan removed his tie, then his jacket, and unbuttoned his white dress shirt. "And we can cover our faces," Ethan said. "We also need to protect our clean air as much as possible."

Ethan was always prepared during scary situations, like the time he and Tyler got Tyler's dad's car stuck on a sand bar. Ethan had calmly suggested putting something under the back wheels to gain traction—and that had worked. Ethan planned to become a rescue worker someday.

Ethan wrapped his dress shirt around the top of his head. Then he arranged the arms to cover his nose and mouth. He made his red tie into a headband to hold the shirt in place.

"There," Ethan said.

Tyler laughed. "You look like the Karate Kid."

"Just call me 'Sensei,'" Ethan joked, flipping the ends of the tie behind his head and standing on one foot with his arms raised. He crane-kicked a leg toward the storm. The smoky cloud looked to be less than a mile away now.

"Can you breathe under all those clothes, Sensei?"

"Yes." Ethan's voice was muffled. "I'll be able to breathe just fine when that dust bomb drops on us."

He pulled out a pair of sunglasses from his jacket pocket. "If you have sunglasses, you can wear them to protect your eyes too."

Everyone else got to work on their own face coverings. It didn't take them long to copy Ethan's method. Not everyone had sunglasses, but some students wrapped their ties around their eyebrows to serve as a windshield of sorts.

"Hey," Ethan said, surveying everyone. "Where's L.J.?"

Then they looked down Interstate 10.

L.J. was in the distance, running away from the storm.

4

Mr. Dwyer cupped a hand around his mouth. "L.J.—get back here! Now!"

It was no use. Even if L.J. decided to listen to their coach, he probably couldn't hear Mr. Dwyer yelling over the approaching wind. The coach took a few running steps as if to chase after L.J. before stuttering to a stop. He glanced back and forth between L.J.'s disappearing form and the rest of the students standing by the bus, looking torn over whether he should follow L.J. or stay with the others.

Tyler shook his head. "Idiot."

Mr. Dwyer's face reddened as he finally walked back to them. "That's just great." He removed his hat and ran his hands through his hair. "He thinks he can outrun the storm." L.J. looked smaller now that he was even farther away.

"Someone needs to go get him," Ethan said.

"No one is going to get him." Mr. Dwyer crossed his arms. "Everyone stays here. It's important for us all to stay together. Is that clear?"

Murmurs of agreement rippled through the group. Sha'relle rolled her eyes.

"*None* of you have service?" Mr. Dwyer tried again. "Someone try texting him—see if that goes through."

Ethan typed out a quick message on his phone, watching it for a minute before he finally looked up with a frown and shook his head to the coach. "Still can't go through."

"He could get heat exhaustion or come across a rattler or get hurt from running in the dust." Mr. Dwyer paused. "He could even die out there. What was he thinking?"

Tyler swallowed. His throat was getting dryer the longer they were stuck out there.

Everyone usually brought water bottles for the tournament, but his bottle was already half-empty. Did anyone else have water left?

"I say it's his own fault for being stupid," José said.

Everyone watched L.J.

Tyler wondered if L.J. might turn around and come back, but he kept getting smaller in the distance.

"Man, why did he have to be so stubborn?" Ethan groaned.

Mr. Dwyer scratched his beard again and rotated his hat in his hands. His face went from red to pink as he calmed down and said, "Let's hope he comes to his senses." He took a few more steps down the highway again before stopping himself like he had before. It seemed like he'd finally come to terms with staying put. He climbed back on the bus, followed by the majority of the team.

As soon as his back was turned, a smaller group of students huddled up.

"We can't just leave him out there," Ethan said. "He doesn't have anything with him—all his stuff is still on the bus. He could run into trouble or collapse in the middle of nowhere, with no one to help him."

"But you heard Mr. Dwyer. He said no else goes," Daniela said.

"He also said it's important we stay together," Ethan said. "So we'll just send two people together." He grinned at his own cleverness.

"You're twisting his words," Daniela said. "You know that's not what he meant. I'm staying here."

"Me too," Sha'relle said.

"Do we have any volunteers for the mission?" Ethan asked. "Anyone?"

No one else moved for a minute.

A few people glanced back at the dust clouds. Sha'relle chewed her thumbnail. Then Julia reluctantly raised her hand.

"I'll do it."

"Great. Thanks, Julia."

Julia was going!

"I'll go too," Tyler said.

"No." Ethan swatted at him to lower his

hand. "You have asthma. You can't run in this weather."

"Okay, fine. I'll go with her," Sha'relle said with a sigh.

Tyler interrupted. "I have my inhaler and a bottle of water," he said. "I can do it. I know I can." Tyler stopped talking and glanced away for a moment. He didn't want to sound too anxious.

Ethan was thinking.

"Besides," Tyler added, "I think sending a guy *and* a girl is a good idea. In case we need to carry L.J. back. No offense, Sha'relle."

Sha'relle took a step back. "None taken. I'm not lifting him. Go for it."

Ethan took in a deep breath and then said, "Okay. We'll need to distract Mr. Dwyer. Some of us will go talk to him, and the rest of us can block his view." He looked at Tyler and Julia. "When the coast looks clear, get going."

5

Tyler snuck onto the bus to grab his backpack, then ducked off and around to the side of the bus where Mr. Dwyer couldn't see.

Tyler pulled on his sunglasses. Julia used her own glasses as eye protection.

Before Tyler put the covering over his face, he shook his inhaler to take one preventative puff. He removed the cap and exhaled all of his breath. *Whoosh!* Then he inhaled, held his breath to the count of ten, and exhaled.

He and Julia wetted down their dress shirts with a small amount of water, then put on the makeshift masks so their faces were completely covered. The wet clothes felt good in the dry, dusty heat.

"How do I look?" Julia asked teasingly. Her entire face was covered in her pale blue dress shirt, so she was left wearing her skirt and a tank top. Tyler could only make out her eyes from behind the clear lenses of her glasses.

"Awesome," Tyler couldn't help saying.

"Get back as soon as possible without overexerting yourselves. Just walk at a decent pace," Ethan instructed. "You don't want to get heatstroke."

"We'll be careful," Julia promised.

José and Kevin were the lookouts, making sure Mr. Dwyer's view was blocked. Daniela and Sha'relle got back in the bus and asked Mr. Dwyer more questions about dust storms. They stood behind his seat so he would have his back to the direction the L.J. rescue party had gone. It wasn't difficult to get Mr. Dwyer talking. In physics class the students liked to ask questions to get Mr. Dwyer going off on tangents, keeping him from giving his weekly pop quizzes.

Tyler and Julia set off at a brisk pace, following the highway like L.J. had. They walked in silence, about a foot apart from each other. Their shoes kicked up dust.

"Good thing we're covered," Julia said. "Especially you, Freckles." She nudged Tyler's pale arm. Julia's dark skin made her less susceptible to sunburn. By her tone of voice, Tyler could tell she was smiling. That made the heat bearable.

Maybe he should ask Julia to the dance right now. If he did ask her now, though, she might think he was opportunistic—that he'd only volunteered to go on the rescue mission so that he could be alone with her. And okay, that was kind of true. But he also just liked being around her. He should at least try to make conversation.

"I wonder how far he got," Tyler said.

"Well, he's been out of sight for a while." Julia glanced at Tyler. Her voice sounded off. She was nervous. "Guess we'll find out when we catch up to him."

Tyler looked back. The sky behind the bus kept turning darker, with the dust storm growing closer every moment. Tyler picked up his pace and Julia sped up to match his stride. He tried to think of another conversation topic to distract her.

"My dad said the drought this year is the worst one in a long time." He cringed. Why did he say that? He bit his lips to prevent any other stupid comments from escaping.

"Yeah," she said.

"We're going to make it, you know," Tyler continued. "We're going to be okay."

She didn't answer for a few moments. Then she said, "I know." They kept walking for a while before she asked, "Do you think we'll run into coyotes?"

"They've probably found their own shelter already. Animals can sense things. When we had Daisy, she sometimes whimpered before the tornado sirens went off."

"Do you still have her?"

"No. She had to be put down last year. Old age."

"I'm sorry." Julia touched his forearm.

"Thanks," Tyler said. "My dad won't let me get another dog right now." He didn't want to get into how his parents had separated about eight months ago and could barely stand to look at each other anymore, let alone have a civilized conversation. Tyler realized that it was unlikely they'd be getting back together, but at this point he would be happy if they could at least stop bickering in front of him.

Julia seemed to notice his sudden change in mood and asked him another question about Daisy. Tyler told her stories about his family dog for nearly a half hour. They passed a few acacia trees. They weren't large enough to provide shade if he and Julia needed it.

A little farther ahead, among the tiny buckthorn bushes along the side of the road, a large boulder loomed along the highway. It stood about a foot shorter than Tyler—and he thought he saw movement near it.

"It looks like there's something behind that boulder." He pointed at a rounded figure— someone crouching down.

"What if it's a coyote?" Julia whispered and stopped.

"It's probably not. And coyotes don't usually attack people. Come on."

When they came around the corner, a sliver of shade leaned away from the boulder. L.J. was crouched in that shade, wedging himself inside the crevice between the boulder and the ground, hiding from the sun.

"What are you doing?" Tyler asked.

L.J. panted and clutched his right ankle as if he was in pain. "I twisted my ankle."

"You shouldn't have run in those dress shoes," Tyler snapped. "You need to think more before just taking off like that. You could have gotten yourself killed—and us. We had to come save you!"

"I know, I know. Can you please spare me the lecture and help me up?"

"Um, we just came all this way to get you, so . . . you're welcome," Tyler said, crossing his arms.

L.J. rubbed his sore ankle and then looked up. "Thanks," he mumbled finally. "Thank you for coming to find me."

Tyler exhaled. "No problem."

"We need to get back," Julia said. "Mr. Dwyer doesn't know we left to find you. Here." She held her hand out to L.J. "I'll help you up. Put your arm around my shoulder."

L.J. pushed himself up, one hand using the boulder, the other hand grasping Julia's hand.

Tyler went over to L.J.'s other side, so L.J. could put an arm around each of them. Tyler didn't want Julia to think he was a jerk.

"Try and rest more of your weight on me," Tyler said, trying not to feel jealous that L.J. had an arm wrapped around Julia. "Come on. Mr. Dwyer has probably figured out we're gone by now, so we need to pick up the pace."

"I hope we're not in too much trouble," Julia said.

L.J. was finally in a standing position. "Okay, I'm ready. Let's go."

***

Hiking back seemed to take longer than the walk to the rock, now that they had been out in the hot sun. Tyler really wanted to drink the water left in his bottle, but he knew he might need it later on. So he tried not to think about his thirst. He also wanted to get back because he had already screwed things up for the team once and didn't want to get in more trouble for disobeying their coach. He hoped Mr. Dwyer would understand once they brought L.J. back safe.

Tyler got a sick feeling as they moved toward the dust clouds, but he knew trying to run away from the storm would be a worse idea. Taking shelter on the bus was their best chance.

Fifteen minutes later, they returned to the bus. L.J. was limping, with an arm still around each of their shoulders. Brown dirt and dust layered over the protective clothes covering Tyler and Julia's faces. *Twenty-five miles per hour.* That was the average speed Ethan said the storm would travel, but this wind felt faster than that.

José and Kevin were screwing around, running outside the bus and kicking up sand.

Everyone else was inside. Ethan, Daniela, and Sha'relle ran out to greet them. Mr. Dwyer came down the steps with a disapproving look on his face.

"As the adult responsible for your safety, I expect you to listen to me when I give you instructions." He gripped his hat in his hands. He was mostly looking at L.J., but then he glanced at Julia and Tyler briefly.

"Sorry," Julia and Tyler said together.

"You were right," L.J. said, limping to a stop in front of Mr. Dwyer. "I'm sorry."

"L.J. twisted his ankle." Julia's voice became clearer as she pulled her mask away from her face.

"Are you sure he wasn't faking just so he could hold onto you?" Ethan teased.

Tyler clenched his fists. Why couldn't L.J. like Daniela or Sha'relle or anyone else?

L.J. whispered something.

"What?" Ethan asked.

"He said, 'Water,'" Julia replied.

"Oh, you're dehydrated? Way to go!" Daniela said sarcastically. "Guess you didn't think about that before you took off."

L.J.'s hair was caked in sweat and dirt. "I'm sorry," he croaked. He sounded like he meant it.

"You're not going to drink all the water we have left," Daniela said.

"Leave him alone," Ethan said. "We'll ration the water."

"Fine." Tyler handed over his water bottle to L.J., who gulped the last of what was there.

"Okay now. Let's not start fighting," Mr. Dwyer said. "We need to move past this. No more runaways. We stay together as a team, deal?"

The students standing outside nodded, some of them looking more comfortable with this plan than others.

"When is the replacement bus going to get here?" Daniela asked. "I have to go to the bathroom."

"They probably aren't letting any buses or emergency vehicles drive in the storm. It's not safe," Mr. Dwyer said.

"Just go outside," José replied to Daniela.

"Yeah, right. Easy for you to say," she snapped.

The clouds were clearly moving closer. The dust storm was less than a football field away.

"At least our bus will cool down once the clouds block the sun," José said.

"Way to find the silver lining. No pun intended." Kevin snorted to himself, and José chuckled. They seemed like the only two people still in a good mood about this situation.

"Everyone back on the bus—let's go," Mr. Dwyer said. "The dust storm will be on top of us any minute."

6

"Did you just bump my leg?" Julia asked Tyler.

"No. How could I have bumped your leg from way over here?" Tyler's face heated up where he was now sitting across the aisle from Julia, several rows back from his seat. "Why?"

"I just . . . I thought I felt something brush it. Never mind."

Tyler wondered if he had lost points with her on the rescue-the-runaway mission. Maybe he shouldn't have talked so much.

"Did you guys see something move?" L.J. shouted.

"What are you talking about?" Daniela asked.

"I didn't see anything," Sha'relle said, ducking her head to peer underneath her seat.

Then someone two rows behind Julia yelled, "Snake! Oh my god!"

Daniela screamed. "Someone get it!" She was up on her seat and looking down at the bus floor.

Several other students climbed onto their seats, even trying to balance on the back part of the seat. Others gasped and squealed.

"Get it out of here!" Daniela shouted.

"I do not like snakes," Tyler muttered to himself, also climbing up on his seat but trying not to look too scared because Julia was right there.

Toward the middle of the bus, Sha'relle held up what looked like a thin rope. "You mean this?" The snake moved and flicked its tongue.

Daniela, who was right beside Sha'relle, screeched.

"Calm down. You'll scare him," Sha'relle said.

"How do you know it's a boy?" José asked.

"It's a harmless garter snake." Sha'relle held it up. The snake was about eighteen inches long and skinny, less than an inch in diameter. She lifted the snake overhead and placed it around her neck.

Daniela gasped as the tan and green scaly animal lay against Sha'relle's dark skin.

"God! What are you doing? How can you hold that thing?" Ethan asked. "You could get bitten!"

"Get it out of here!" Daniela pleaded.

Sha'relle let go of the snake and let it wrap around her upper arm.

"How can you touch that slimy thing?" Daniela asked.

"Snakes aren't slimy. They're not even wet—we're in the desert. I think they're cool. Aren't you, little buddy?" Sha'relle held the head of the snake near her face and talked to it. She petted its little head as its tongue darted in and out.

"God. You're freaking me out!" Daniela squealed.

"Garter snakes aren't even venomous," Sha'relle pointed out.

Daniela shook her head. "I don't care what you say. That is nasty."

"My mom has snakeskin boots," Kevin offered, as if that would comfort her.

"Just get it out of here." Daniela shooed a hand in the air and made a disgusted face.

"It must have gotten on the bus when the front door was left open," Mr. Dwyer suggested. "Let's shut the door before we get any more animal stowaways."

The bus driver slammed the door shut and the panels shook in their hinges. He pressed against them to make sure they were secure. The rattling stopped.

"Please. Get it out of here." Daniela held up her hand, scooting away from Sha'relle. "Just. Please."

"You're hurting his feelings," Sha'relle joked.

"Whatever," Daniela scoffed.

"Come on," Mr. Dwyer said. "Toss it out the window."

"Sheesh. Fine." Sha'relle walked over to an open window. "They just don't understand you," she said to the garter snake. "So long, little friend."

Tyler glanced at Julia. Her arms were folded tight, hugging her middle.

Sha'relle unwrapped the snake from her arm. She reached toward the window and dropped the snake through the narrow opening, and as soon as it landed, it slithered away on the sand.

The dust storm was now less than half a football field away.

7

"Now that everyone is *on* the bus . . . " Mr.
Dwyer raised an eyebrow in L.J.'s direction.
L.J. sank down in his seat. "And all critters
are, hopefully, *off* the bus . . . " He shot a look
at Sha'relle, who just smiled and brushed her
hands together.

"We need to get ready," Mr. Dwyer
continued. "The bus needs to be as airtight
as possible. Close all the windows. Look
for any cracks in the seams and fill them
with . . . something, anything."

The team stood there, dumbfounded, for
a moment.

"You heard him," Ethan said. "Close up

all the windows. *Hurry.*" Most of the students leapt into action.

But Kevin and José leaned back and put their feet up on the seatbacks in front of them. Ethan yanked Kevin's legs down. "Not cool," he said. "Both of you, get up and help."

Kevin gave him a dirty look and then got up reluctantly. José followed.

The sound of windows sliding up and clicking closed resonated through the bus.

Tyler's window was open too. He pushed the metal latches inward and heaved up, but the window was stuck halfway.

"Come on, come *on.*" Tyler slapped at the window—then rubbed his stinging hand. He pushed on the metal latches again, but they wouldn't budge. "Come. *On.*" He slammed the heel of his hand into it. Why hadn't the others thought about this while he and Julia were out looking for L.J.?

The dust cloud grew closer. Tyler had never seen anything like it. A wall of black and brown clouds churned toward them. It looked like photos he had seen of bombs being dropped in a war.

Tyler pounded and pushed at the metal window latch. Finally–*Click*—it gave way and slid up a notch. He pushed the latches inward again and pushed the window closed. It clicked into place. "There." He brushed off his hands.

Four guys, including José and Kevin, fought to see out the back of the bus's emergency-door window and watch the approaching storm. But the rest of the team continued checking windows.

"No, that's okay," Julia yelled sarcastically toward the slackers watching out the back window. "We got it. No need to help. We're fine."

Mr. Dwyer hurried around the bus, checking all the windows one more time. Another window wouldn't close and it was already letting in dust and wind.

"Keep your coverings around your faces. You need to protect your nose and mouth," Mr. Dwyer said.

"Why do we need to do that if we're inside the bus?" Kevin asked.

"Because dust could still leak in." Mr. Dwyer's voice had never sounded more tense. "It's a precaution."

"I can't get this one closed!" José shouted from a seat toward the back, where he'd finally moved to get to the last window. "Can somebody help me?"

"I got it," Kevin said, coming over to José. His fingers turned white where he pressed into the locks. He heaved. "Ugh! Never mind. It won't budge."

"Let me try," Ethan offered, leaning over the seat to reach for the window.

"Get something to cover it with," Mr. Dwyer suggested. Kids scrambled and dug through their backpacks.

"I have a sweatshirt!" Kevin said, while Sha'relle offered a hat she'd found.

"Use my jacket." Ethan grabbed his black sport coat. The upper window was stuck halfway open, just a few inches high but about a foot wide. It was a big enough hole to let in more than a little dust once the storm hit the bus.

"We have to get that opening covered or we could have sand all over the bus," Mr. Dwyer instructed.

"It's just sand," José said.

"Have you ever breathed in sand?" Mr. Dwyer asked.

"No."

"*Or* gotten a tiny piece of sand in your eyes?" Mr. Dwyer added.

"Oh, yeah. It stung."

"Well, try getting a dozen tiny particles in your eyes," Mr. Dwyer said. "Your cornea could get scratched."

José quickly dug through his backpack and found a sleep mask he'd brought. "Ha!" he shouted, holding the mask above his head.

Ethan shook his head. "You are lucky."

"I'm prepared," José corrected with a grin. He strapped the sleep mask onto his forehead like a pair of goggles.

"Right. Prepared to sleep," Ethan said before returning his attention to the open window.

"How can we secure this?" Mr. Dwyer asked.

"Here," the bus driver said, walking down the aisle. He looked out of breath just from walking that short distance. His round belly hung over his belt. Being a bus driver involved a lot of sitting and probably wasn't the best occupation for staying in shape, Tyler reflected.

"Use this duct tape. I always carry it with me." The driver handed Ethan a roll of tape and huffed back to his seat, where he tried to call for help on his radio again.

No one answered.

José held the jacket up to the window and Ethan peeled off the thick, gray tape and secured the cloth over the hole. Everyone was silent on the bus. Some watched Ethan and José secure the jacket, while others were staring out their own windows. The bus had begun to rock slightly from the wind, and it sounded like stones and sand were pelting the sides.

"Look!" Julia squeezed Tyler on the arm.

They both looked outside. The cactus that

had been bent at a forty-five-degree angle minutes ago had shifted to a ninety-degree angle—all the way sideways.

8

"**D**oes that look like a twenty-five-mile-an-hour wind to you?" Tyler shouted as the wind began to rattle the bus even harder.

"Twenty-five is the average," Ethan explained. "Dust storms can move faster."

The driver locked the doors and turned off all the bus lights. Tyler figured he did that as a safety precaution. He remembered the firefighter safety speaker saying this prevented other cars from seeing the headlights and misjudging where the bus was on the road.

Pull aside. Stay alive. Tyler hoped if anyone came along on the highway, they would know to do that in a dust storm *and* not accidentally hit the bus.

"The sky's all black and gray, smoky-looking," L.J. said. "Like something big exploded, like Chernobyl."

"I think you mean Hiroshima," Ethan said.

Of course Ethan would know to correct him. Ethan loved history. Did L.J. even know that about him? *A good friend would know things like that*, Tyler thought.

"But it's not quite like the photos of Hiroshima," Ethan went on. "That explosion looked more like a cauliflower, and you could see the top of it where the smoke ended, but this dust cloud looks a mile wide. See how it takes over the sky?"

The enormous gray cloud rolled toward them, as thick as pollution from a factory.

"How can a dust cloud get that big?" L.J. asked. Everyone looked to Mr. Dwyer.

"Well, the strong winds cause a downdraft in an area of land with sand or topsoil," Mr. Dwyer explained, going into teaching-mode. "So the dirt and sand lifts right off the ground—sometimes up as high as five hundred feet and a mile wide. Experts call these storms black blizzards because the dust clouds get so dark."

"What do we do once it gets here?" Julia asked.

"Yeah, what else can we do to protect ourselves?" Ethan said, looking expectantly at their teacher. "We don't have much time."

Mr. Dwyer scratched his beard again. "Well, we've already covered up," he started. "I think all we can do now is sit tight and hope for the best."

The cloud drew closer, but it moved slowly, kicking more dust and dirt into the air. The light from the afternoon sun was getting blocked out more and more.

Tyler's ears popped again. Then he heard a high-pitched howling noise in the distance.

"What was that?" Julia asked, clutching at her seat as she tried to peer out the windows. "It sounded like a coyote."

"It was just the wind," Tyler told her. It had to be the wind.

The bus swayed and creaked. Dirt and debris began smacking the sides of the bus and the windows. The eerie darkness kept rolling toward them like a fog.

Tyler had once gone to a football game at the University of Phoenix stadium, where the Cardinals played, and the way that retractable roof slowly opened up was kind of how the dust storm moved. But the stadium's retractable roof didn't get right in your face and burn your eyes and throw debris at you.

Then, all at once, the cloud was upon them—and they were shrouded in darkness.

9

The dust cloud completely blocked the sun, making it look like nighttime inside the bus. The cloud was like an eclipse, but it didn't just cover the circle of the sun like a solar eclipse did. The dust clouds covered the entire sky. Everyone grew quiet.

"I can't believe how dark it is," Sha'relle whispered. "You can't see a thing!"

"The cloud is completely covering us," Daniela said.

Dust and dirt whirled around them, pelting the bus and sounding like a BB gun shooting at aluminum cans.

The jacket covering the open window

billowed inward like a sail on a ship. Tyler watched it carefully. If that blazer blew off, they would have dust and dirt everywhere inside the bus. José kneeled on his seat to press down on the tape and make sure it stayed secure.

Kevin walked to the front of the bus and sat across from where Mr. Dwyer was sitting behind the bus driver.

"Got any good jokes?" Kevin asked, pushing his shirt-covering away from his face so it sat on top of his head like a hood.

"Seriously?" Mr. Dwyer turned to him in surprise. "You're not worried about the storm?"

"Nah—it'll pass," Kevin said. "I was in a dust storm once at the mall. We just stayed inside. It blew over after a while. It was just super dark. Like this."

"Well, okay then. Let's see . . . " Mr. Dwyer scratched his beard. "Oh, here's one."

Kevin leaned forward. This was the most he'd paid attention all day. Some of the other students on the bus stopped fidgeting so they could listen too. Mr. Dwyer's jokes were famously lame, but apparently everyone could go for a distraction right now.

"Mr. Neutron walks into an IHOP and says, 'I'm starving. How much for a stack of pancakes?' The waitress says, 'For you, Mr. Neutron, no charge.'"

Kevin laughed and shook his head. Corny as usual.

At a sudden gust of wind, one panel of the front door flew open. It was the side that had been rattling earlier.

The dirt and dust hit Kevin first. He yelped and scrambled to cover his face, which was now unprotected.

From what Tyler could see—which wasn't much in the darkened bus—Kevin was bent over on his seat and holding his head. The driver jumped to get to the door and Mr. Dwyer was already out of his seat, crouching in front of Kevin to look at his face.

"I got dust in my eyes!" Kevin groaned.

The driver fought against the wind to push the door closed. He pounded a fist against it until it finally snapped shut. Tyler could feel his heart begin to race.

"Someone hand me that duct tape," the driver shouted. "Quick! Hand me the tape!"

Ethan ran up with the tape, tearing off a long strip. The driver pressed it against the panel.

"More!"

Ethan pulled off another strip, and the driver plastered that one on too. They worked with a system, Ethan tearing the tape and the driver hastily attaching it to the panel as rapidly as they could.

"That should hold it," the driver finally exhaled, exhausted.

"How much water do we have? Who has water left?" Mr. Dwyer asked, keeping his eyes on Kevin where he had curled up onto his seat.

Three students, including Julia, rushed to the front of the bus with water bottles.

Their coach grabbed Julia's bottle first. "Kevin, we need to flush out your eyes. Here—cup your hands and I'll pour some water."

Kevin squinted as he cupped his hands and Mr. Dwyer poured some water. Then Kevin splashed the water into his eyes to clear them. Mr. Dwyer refilled Kevin's cupped hands several times.

"That's better," Kevin said after a while. "It's getting better."

The door was closed, but the damage was already done. Dust had floated inside, coating the air so it felt gritty and thicker than before.

Tyler's heart was still pounding and he was starting to have trouble catching his breath. He coughed, and then wheezed, grabbing at his chest. He knew this feeling. He last had it during gym when they played indoor hockey. Tyler had been running toward the goal and suddenly felt like his throat constricted. He'd had to use his inhaler that day. It took three puffs of the medicine to get his breathing under control. Struggling for breath was the worst feeling ever. He felt so helpless.

This was the same feeling. The coughing. The wheezing. The constricted throat. An asthma attack was coming on.

10

"Can't . . . breathe." Tyler held his chest. He tried to inhale, but the air stopped, as though a valve on his throat had been shut and nothing was allowed through. The students were supposed to keep their faces covered, especially after what just happened to Kevin, but Tyler yanked his dress shirt away from his head and pushed his sunglasses onto his forehead.

He worked his way up the aisle toward the seat where his backpack sat. He was wheezing badly now, grabbing the hard foam seat cushions to stay steady on his feet.

"Tyler, are you okay?" Julia asked with wide eyes.

Tyler shook his head but kept moving. In the dim light, everything was confusing. His eyes adjusted a little, but all the seats looked the same.

The light inside the bus was now reddish as the dust and dirt moved through the area. The whole bus had a post-apocalyptic look to it.

"What's wrong with him?" a freshman girl asked. Her face looked distorted in the ruddy light. Tyler felt like he was in a freaky funhouse where the mirrors warped everything.

"I think it's his asthma," Ethan said.

Finally, Tyler reached his seat. He grabbed his backpack and hauled it up on the seat. He struggled to unzip the stupid thing and dug through the contents—phone, granola bar, speech notes—looking for the one thing that he needed.

Then he remembered it was in a side pocket, but there were like a dozen side pockets. He squeezed the canvas outside of the pack until he hit something solid. *There!* He dragged the zipper around the curves of the pocket and felt inside. *Got it!*

Tyler shook the inhaler and flipped off the top to remove the cap. Then he stuck it in his mouth, exhaled what little air was left in him, and pressed down. *Whoosh.* He inhaled deeply and held his breath to the count of ten.

He exhaled and almost instantly felt relief. His throat opened. He could breathe. He coughed. He shook the inhaler again and took another puff. *Whoosh.* He inhaled deeply and counted to ten again.

Even better.

"Hey! Something's wrong with Daniela!" someone shouted from the front of the bus, near where the door had blown open. "Someone help her!"

Daniela's breath was quickening. "I feel dizzy!" she wheezed. "I feel dizzy!"

"I think she's hyperventilating!" Sha'relle shouted. "Is she having an asthma attack too?"

"No—wait!" said Ethan. "It looks more like she's having a panic attack."

Mr. Dwyer was still helping Kevin, so Ethan came to Daniela's side and grasped her shoulders. "You're okay. Just breathe. You're okay," he said. "Does anyone have a paper bag?"

Ethan breathed slowly with her while the others searched their belongings. The bus was dark, so everything happened in the shadows.

Julia ran over with an empty lunch bag in her hand. "Here!"

Ethan handed the bag to Daniela. "Here. Breathe into this—deep breaths."

The dust storm kept pelting the bus with debris. *Ping. Ping. Ping.*

Daniela held the bag to her face and the bag expanded and contracted.

"Good, good," Ethan coached her until she calmed down. "Better now?"

Daniela nodded. "Yeah," she said, her voice muffled by the paper bag, which inflated and deflated with her breathing. "I'm okay."

Mr. Dwyer stood up from Kevin's seat. "You're doing great, guys. Everything's going to be fine."

The ruddy sky still colored the light a reddish brown. Tyler squinted to check his watch. He'd lowered his sunglasses to protect his eyes again, but they were virtually impossible to see through with the sky this dark.

It was 5:22 p.m. The sky kept shifting colors. Red, brown, black, red again. The team would have been home by now if it weren't for the dust storm. Tyler and his dad would have been firing up the grill and cooking some burgers, getting ready to watch the game.

"Keep your faces covered," Ethan warned everyone. "The air in here is compromised."

The eerie, fog-like dust hung in the air around the bus. Colors shifted every few minutes as pillows of dust washed over them.

Julia slipped next to Tyler in his seat. She squeezed his hand and his heart did a one-eighty flip. She even interlaced their fingers. He couldn't believe he wasn't dreaming this. She hadn't let go of his hand yet. The whole thing felt surreal.

Tyler squeezed back to make sure he was really awake. Then he worried his hand might get sweaty. That would be gross. After a while, Tyler gently let go of her hand.

Someone began to cry.

"Are we going to die?" Daniela whispered.

"Don't be stupid. We'll be fine," Sha'relle shushed her.

"No one's going to die," Ethan said, but his voice sounded shaky as if he didn't quite believe what he was saying.

"I need to get out of here!" It was Daniela again. She bolted out of her seat and raced toward the back emergency exit. "I'm getting out!"

"No," Ethan said, following her. "Calm down. Take deep breaths. You're okay, Daniela." He took her hand and led her back to her seat, but stood in the aisle in between her and the emergency exit. Mr. Dwyer was now standing near the front entrance, so they didn't have to worry about her trying that door.

The wind outside howled more loudly than ever, continuing to rock the bus like waves against a ship. The storm continued to swirl along its path toward Phoenix and tossed debris against the side of the bus. The other students were still rustling with nervous energy. Someone was still crying. Ethan was so good at helping keep people calm, but what if too many people started panicking at once? Tyler felt he had to do something to help keep the tension in check. Then he had an idea.

Tyler stood in the center of the aisle. Standing was supposed to help project the voice. He adjusted the shirt covering his face. He needed to keep using it as a protection against the dust, even though the covering muffled his voice. In order for his voice to be heard all the way to the back of the bus, he'd need to speak up. Tyler cleared his throat. Having the first sentence memorized and ready to deliver was key to a successful speech.

"There is a story of a rabbit's foot that allowed anyone who possessed it to make three wishes."

The crying ceased and ended with a sniffle.

The bus looked like a theater of silhouettes. The shadows appeared to look up at him. There was a trickle of noise as people quieted down and shifted in their seats.

Sha'relle whispered, "It's his story. His event."

"*Shhhh*," Ethan hissed.

Tyler straightened up. He was off to a good start, much better than during the competition. In competitions, the students always had microphones, but speaking with microphones made him nervous—especially when they made that awful feedback sound like Tyler's microphone had earlier that day. The darkness helped keep Tyler's fear of failure at bay, but right now his goal wasn't to win an event. If he did a good job, maybe he could help people forget about the storm for a while.

The details of the story poured out easily: how the rabbit's foot wound up in an old woman's hands, how she wished to have her dead husband back, how she wished to be young again.

The bus was swaying in the wind and Tyler steadied himself by grasping the seatbacks. By the time he reached the end of the story, he was gesturing with his hands and hardly considering the storm outside.

"And that is how Abigail's Rabbit's Foot taught her to be careful what she wished for."

The bus was silent for a few moments. Then someone clapped. The applause was coming from where Tyler thought Ethan was sitting, but pretty soon everyone else joined in. Tyler took a bow, even though people couldn't really see him. He remembered what his dad said again: *You appreciate things more if you have to earn them.* And Tyler felt he had earned this applause. He had delivered a great speech to a captive audience, and suddenly the tournament results didn't seem to matter as much. He enjoyed the feeling of triumph until the wind howled.

The howling really did sound like a coyote, and it brought everyone back to the situation at hand. The bus creaked and rattled again.

Thunk!

Something big and heavy hit a side window and shattered the glass. Was it a bird? A rock? Tyler couldn't tell. Voices shouted in the darkness.

"Oh my god!" Daniela yelped. "Our window!"

"Stay calm," Sha'relle reminded her. "I need a sweater or something." Footsteps stampeded to the front of the bus, then back again.

Kevin handed his sweatshirt to José, who carried it over to the girls. "Thanks," Sha'relle said quickly. She turned to Daniela. "Help me hold this in place. Someone get the tape!"

"Here," Mr. Dwyer said, handing Sha'relle the roll of duct tape as she pressed the sweatshirt against the window.

Tyler rushed to the girls' window and fought to hold one side of the sweatshirt down. A sleeve of the sweatshirt flapped up and smacked Tyler in the face. He pushed it down again with his free hand. Something sharp bit his hand. He jerked his hand away.

José held the sweatshirt in place at the other end of the window. Sha'relle taped the fabric in place just like they'd done with the other window.

More dust had blown in through the broken window. Now the air in the bus was even worse. Once the covering was in place, Tyler stepped away. He felt something wet on his hand—but it wasn't raining.

He sniffed his hand where he had felt the sting. Blood—he smelled blood.

"I think I cut myself!" Tyler said. "I need to stop the bleeding."

"Don't panic. We need to find some fabric to press down on it," Mr. Dwyer instructed, looking through the seats.

Julia hastily untied a decorative scarf she kept looped through the strap on her messenger bag. She rushed over and wound the scarf around his hand several times. "Press down where it's bleeding," Mr. Dwyer said again.

Julia gripped Tyler's hand and pressed the wound with him.

"You're going to be fine. You'll be okay." She kept repeating herself. "Everything's going to be okay."

Tyler took slow, deep breaths, trying to stay calm so his asthma wouldn't act up again.

Breathebreathebreathe . . . breathe . . . breathe. . . . . . breathe . . . . breathe.

He prayed he wouldn't have another asthma attack. What if the inhaler didn't work next time?

12

White light began to filter through the dust cloud, which was starting to break apart. A thinner cloud remained, reminding Tyler of a thick fog. The cloud was passing on.

After the dust broke up and seemed to continue moving toward Phoenix, the bus driver peeled the duct tape off the front door so everyone could get out.

"Kevin, how are your eyes?" Mr. Dwyer coughed.

"They're better—thanks." That was the most serious Tyler had ever seen Kevin.

They stepped outside and Mr. Dwyer

coughed some more. Tyler stepped toward him. "Mr. Dwyer . . . ?"

The coach held up a hand. "I'm okay," he said. "I just need a minute." He bent over, resting his hands on his knees.

The terrain was different after the storm. Sand dunes had formed where the wind lifted dust and rock off the ground. The grouping of cacti that had been bent over before stood up straighter, but they were partially buried in a foot of sand that had blown against them.

The wheels of the bus were covered in sand too. They would need to be dug out whenever the bus was rescued. The sides of the bus had taken the worst beating. They were dimpled with tiny dents, as if they'd developed freckles like Tyler's. A layer of sand and dirt covered the outside of the bus as if the team had gone joy riding in the muddy backwoods. But being stuck in that dust storm had been no joy ride.

As the bus driver stepped down off of the bus, he was winded and sweating again. The air was still dry—and still full of dust and dirt particles. But the storm had actually lowered the temperature . . . so why was the bus driver still sweating so much? Tyler was glad *he* didn't sweat quite that much or he'd have to keep an extra can of deodorant in his locker to get through the school day.

The driver looked like he was having a hard time breathing now. He coughed and wheezed, falling to his knees as his face turned pale.

"What's wrong with him?" José asked.

Mr. Dwyer rushed over to the driver. "I think it's a heart attack."

"Oh my god!" Julia's hands flew to cover her mouth.

"Does anyone know CPR?" Mr. Dwyer asked. "I'm having trouble catching my breath."

The driver slumped all the way to the ground. He lay on his side, not moving.

Tyler stared a moment, then shook his head as if waking up from a dream again. He and Ethan had attended a CPR class together last fall, after the firefighter had given his *pull aside, stay alive* talk.

"Yeah," he said. "I do. I know CPR, but I can't do it with my hand like this."

"And because of your asthma attack," Ethan said. "I can do it." But he stood frozen in place, as if he'd completely forgotten what to do.

"I can help," Tyler suggested, remembering that the class's instructor had encouraged people to work in teams. Ethan looked up at him gratefully. Tyler dropped to his knees across from Ethan so the driver lay in between them.

"First," Tyler reminded, "you have to check his breathing."

Ethan leaned down and turned his head so his ear was near the driver's nose and mouth. Then Ethan waited a few seconds to see if he felt the guy breathing.

"Do you feel any air?" Tyler asked.

"No—he's not breathing," Ethan said. "I'm starting CPR."

"I'll help count," Tyler offered.

They'd learned from their CPR class that they were supposed to do chest compressions until the person began breathing again.

Tyler watched as Ethan felt for the breastbone in the middle of the driver's chest. Ethan's hands shook. He interlaced his fingers with the left hand on top of the right hand and the right hand palm down. Then he placed his hands so they covered two inches of the chest bone, the way they'd practice at the class.

Ethan pressed in, doing the first compression. He pushed down hard with the heel of his right hand. Then he followed up with a second and a third compression—more than one per second. Tyler started singing a song quietly under his breath, which the instructor had said would help keep a tempo for the compressions. Ethan picked up on his cue and started humming along. The process looked a lot different on a real person than on the resuscitation doll. And the driver was a big guy.

"You're doing great!" Tyler said, and then kept count. "Five, six, seven, eight . . . " Meanwhile, Mr. Dwyer said, "Sha'relle, see if the radio is working yet."

The driver had tried to radio for help right after the bus had broken down, but the radio hadn't worked with the approaching storm. Maybe it would work now that the air had cleared.

Sha'relle ran up the bus steps and grabbed the radio hand-piece. She pressed the button on the side. "Hello?"

Static crackled in response.

"Try another frequency," Mr. Dwyer yelled.

Sha'relle flipped the knob. Another channel opened up. "Is anyone there? We need help!"

Tyler focused on counting for Ethan, who was still humming under his breath, while Sha'relle finally made contact with someone over the radio.

"They're coming! They're sending an ambulance and another bus," Sha'relle shouted, hanging up the radio and hopping down the steps. The other students cheered.

Suddenly the driver moved. Ethan jumped back as the man coughed and gagged.

"Turn him on his side," Mr. Dwyer said, crouching near them.

Tyler cradled the driver's head while Ethan rolled him over. The driver threw up. His face was grayish and sweaty, but he was breathing. The man was alive.

Julia looked at Ethan and Tyler. "You did it. That was amazing!"

Ethan exhaled and glanced at Tyler. "Couldn't have done it alone."

Julia squeezed Tyler's shoulder.

Tyler's heart was racing again, either from the adrenaline of the moment or from Julia touching his shoulder. He breathed in deeply. The driver was alive. The CPR had worked. Someone was coming to help them. Now Tyler hoped the ambulance would arrive soon. From the looks of the driver's face, which was still as gray as the retreating dust storm, he probably wasn't out of the woods yet.

13

"I see something," Kevin was saying about a half hour later. "Look over there!"

"What is that?" José squinted and stared at the horizon.

In the distance, it looked like something moving. Lights flashed. A faint sound of a siren wailed, but the sound went in and out with the wind.

Was it just a mirage? Or was it like when you see something on a hot day and the sun makes the heat in the air shimmer? Mr. Dwyer had taught them that the effect was called heat haze. Hot air rises and mixes with cool air, distorting the light waves.

The group stood in a line and stared, with their hands up to their foreheads to shield their eyes from the setting sun. From a distance, they probably looked like a company of soldiers saluting. They *had* been like soldiers—like in one of Tyler's video games, but instead of battling an army of zombies, they had battled nature.

The approaching shape came from the opposite direction that the storm had gone.

It was a vehicle, coming down the road from Tucson.

"It's the ambulance," Sha'relle breathed.

Now that it got closer, the siren grew louder. And something else was in the distance further behind the ambulance: the replacement bus.

"They're coming for us!" Ethan shouted. "They're coming for us!"

Tyler and Ethan ran along the side of the bus and drummed their hands against the dimpled metal as they cheered and whooped. It was covered in a layer of dust and dirt and every slap against the side of the bus left smudgy handprints, but they didn't care.

***

When the ambulance got close, some of the students started waving their arms so the vehicle would pull up to where the bus driver was lying on the ground. The back doors of the ambulance opened, and two paramedics jumped out. They brought a stretcher over to the driver.

"What happened?" one paramedic asked as she glanced at the rest of them.

"Heart attack, we think," Mr. Dwyer said. "Some students performed CPR."

The paramedics leaned down and spoke to the driver. "Can you hear me?"

The driver was out of it, but after a moment, he wheezed, "Yes."

"Do you know where you are? What state are we in?"

"Arizona."

"Where were you today?"

The driver paused before responding. He

moaned in pain and touched his chest where Ethan had done the compressions.

"You're probably just sore from the CPR. That's normal," the paramedic said. She kept her voice calm. "Do you remember what you were doing today?"

"Well . . . I drove to a speech tournament . . . in Tucson."

"How are you feeling?"

"Not so good." He struggled to stand up, and his legs wobbled. The paramedic's hands hovered over him.

"Whoa, sir. Let's get you on a gurney."

"That's probably best."

The two paramedics ran back to the ambulance, propped up the legs of the gurney, and rolled it near the driver.

"Lie down flat on your back," the other paramedic instructed as he prepped the gurney once it was stopped.

They stood on either side of the driver, hoisted him onto the gurney, and wheeled him over to the ambulance. Once they'd loaded him into the back, the male paramedic jumped inside. The other closed the doors and then came back to the rest of group.

"Who did the CPR?" she asked.

Everyone pointed at Ethan.

She smiled at him. "You saved this man's life, young man. He should thank his lucky stars you were here."

"Thanks," Ethan said. "But it was a team effort." He jerked a thumb toward Tyler.

A smile tugged the corners of Tyler's mouth. Maybe he wasn't such a screwup after all.

14

Tyler felt lighter somehow. After grabbing his backpack from the old bus, he launched up the steps of the rescue bus that had just arrived—another yellow school bus. He walked halfway down the aisle and slid into a seat. No one had wanted to sit with him on the initial ride home, but now he didn't care. He just wanted to *get* home. He yawned and leaned his head against the window. His stomach growled. He found the granola bar in his backpack and unwrapped it. The first thing he would do when he got home was eat some chips and salsa while his dad grilled burgers for dinner. In the meantime,

Tyler figured he'd probably sleep the whole ride home.

The rest of the team filtered onto the bus and grabbed cold water bottles from a cooler in the first row. They didn't look at all like the clean-cut, suited-up team that had competed at the tournament in Tucson earlier that day. Dust stained their faces. Their clothes hung disheveled and smeared with brown dust and dirt. Some looked like baseball players who had slid into home one too many times. The bus smelled of dry dust and sweat. Tyler couldn't wait to take a shower when he got home.

Julia rushed down the aisle to find a seat, grinning over at Tyler when she passed him. He still didn't have the nerve to ask her to the dance. José, Daniela, and Sha'relle all climbed aboard. L.J. limped by, then Ethan. Tyler purposely stared out the window as Ethan came down the aisle.

Outside, Mr. Dwyer shook hands with the new bus driver. As he climbed aboard, he helped Kevin to a seat. Before leaving, the paramedics had said Kevin would need to see a doctor, but his injuries weren't permanent. They gave him a clean, wet cloth to press against his eyes for the trip back.

Mr. Dwyer stood at the front of the bus with a relieved grin on his face. "We were finally able to contact the school. Your families have all been informed of what happened and are waiting for us to get back."

Daniela held her phone in the air. "I just got service! I'm texting my moms." Several students cheered while others checked their own phones for service.

"Can I sit here?"

Tyler had been so focused on texting his parents as well that he hadn't even noticed Ethan standing in the aisle next to his seat. "Huh?"

"I said, can I sit here?"

"Oh. Uh, sure?" Tyler removed his backpack from the seat beside him and shoved it underneath.

"Thanks." Ethan slid into the seat and stored his bag underneath it too.

They sat in silence for a few minutes as the bus finally took off. Tyler bit his fingernail and glanced out the window.

Eventually Ethan cleared his throat and said, "Everyone screws up, you know?"

"I thought you were mad at me," Tyler replied quietly.

"Mad? Why?"

"You know. For letting the team down."

"Hey, that could have happened to any of us."

"Anyone?" Tyler asked.

They both looked back at L.J. Then they looked at each other for a moment and then cracked up.

"Okay," Ethan admitted. "Anyone but him."

"What about before? You and L.J.—you were laughing and pointing at me."

"What?" Ethan looked at L.J. again and furrowed his eyebrows, trying to remember the earlier conversation. "Oh, that." He swatted a hand in the air. "That wasn't about you. I was asking him about next week's calculus test."

"Really? So you weren't avoiding me?"

"Uh, no. I thought you might want some space on the ride home after what happened." Ethan smiled at the shocked look that must have been all over Tyler's face. "You know, not everything revolves around you."

"I know that." Tyler had gotten himself so bummed out, but they hadn't been making fun of him. They hadn't been talking about him at all.

"Dude, did you really think I would sit there and make fun of you?"

Tyler's cheeks flushed with embarrassment. Instead of answering, he asked, "You up for playing *Injustice* tonight?"

"Ah, nice speech technique: changing the subject. I'd give that a ten for creativity and poise." Ethan grinned again and shook his head at Tyler. "Okay, *Injustice*. Tonight. My house. I'll make the popcorn. You bring the soda."

"Deal. I'll be over after dinner." Tyler felt the corners of his mouth tug upward. They were going to be okay. Even though Tyler had screwed up, he still had his best friend. But he didn't have a date to the dance.

15

When the replacement bus pulled into the school parking lot, the team parents were huddled together, some holding coffee cups. Most of them rushed toward the bus when it approached the curb. Tyler searched the crowd for his mom or dad, looking for either of their cars. He was surprised to see that they were standing together.

The bus stopped and the driver opened the front door. Mr. Dwyer climbed out first and stood outside the bottom of the steps, fist-bumping each student stepping off the bus. Daniela was the first one off the bus. She opened her arms to greet the fresh air.

Sha'relle pushed past her and headed right to her mom. Tyler saw Kevin standing with his grandparents, pointing at his eyes and looking as if he was retelling the incident when storm sand got in his eyes. José walked nonchalantly off the bus, but he rushed over to his dad and step-mom as soon as he saw them. L.J. limped down, his ankle still swollen.

The other kids filtered to their waiting families. Julia, Ethan, and Tyler were the last ones off the bus. Mr. Dwyer held up a fist for Tyler, but then Tyler remembered the painful cut on his hand and fist-bumped with his left one instead.

Tyler's mom and dad hugged him at the same time when he finally made his way over to them. He'd never been so glad to see them. "We're so glad you're all right," said his mom as she hugged him again. "They said over the radio that you helped perform CPR?"

Tyler nodded. "Well, I helped Ethan keep count. I couldn't do the CPR myself because of the asthma . . . and I sort of hurt my hand."

His mom gasped, reaching for the hand still wrapped up in Julia's scarf, which was now covered in dried blood and dust.

"I'm fine, Mom," he insisted. "It's just a scratch."

"You know," his dad said to his mom with a smile, "he's turning into quite the young man—and I'd still say that even if his speech team hadn't gone to the State Championship."

"We've got a pretty great kid," his mom agreed. Tyler felt his mouth spread into a grin again. The joy of seeing his parents getting along gave him a spark of courage. He wanted to catch Julia before she headed home. He quietly ducked away while his parents kept talking.

Tyler searched the crowd. Where was she? Then he spotted her short brown hair and brightly-colored messenger bag. She was walking through the parking lot with her mom.

"Hey, Julia! Wait up!"

She turned around and pushed up her glasses. Even though her hair was disheveled and her clothes were covered in dust, she still looked cute to him.

Tyler jogged across the parking lot.

"Hey," she said, smiling.

"Well, we made it." Tyler shifted nervously on his feet.

"Yeah," she laughed. "We did."

"Come on, Julia," her mom called.

Julia turned and said, "Give me a minute." She sighed and turned back to Tyler. They stood there another moment. Julia chewed her bottom lip.

"How's your hand?" she pointed at his blood-soaked bandage.

"I'll put some antiseptic on it as soon as I get home. I'll be fine. It's already starting to feel better, thanks to your bandage," he said, even though the cut still burned.

"I'm glad," she said, smiling.

"I can get it back to you if you want . . . "

"No, that's okay," Julia lifted her hands and laughed. Tyler had to admit, it was pretty gross now. "I really don't need it."

She kept smiling at him. That had to be a good sign, right?

"Do you like to eat?" Tyler burst out. He shook his head. "I mean, uh, what do you like to eat?"

"Oh. Um. I like Italian. Pizza. Pasta." Julia rocked on her heels. "Why?"

"I thought . . . maybe we could go eat something—together—sometime."

After a moment, she said, "I'd like that." Tyler couldn't help but grin. *So she does like me!* he thought to himself. Julia paused another moment. "Well, I have to go." She motioned toward her mom's car. "My mom's waiting."

Tyler looked around her at her mom, who was watching them. Julia turned and started to leave. *It's now or never.* He mustered his courage.

"Wait!" Tyler said, a little more loud and desperate than he had wanted to sound.

"Yeah?" Julia shifted her bag onto her other shoulder.

Tyler stood there. He scratched the back of his head. "Um . . . " For the second time today, he couldn't find his words. This wasn't at all how he'd wanted this to go. "I'm sorry," he said hastily and laughed. *Well, this isn't going well.*

Julia smiled again and touched his arm. "Would you want to go to Spring Fling together?" she said.

Tyler stood there, dumbfounded. His tongue stuck to the roof of his mouth and his eyebrows shot up.

"We could go with a group," she quickly added. "Two of my friends are already going. It'll be fun!"

Tyler exhaled. "Yeah," he said. He cleared his throat. "Yes, I would love that." He was glad she hadn't said they could just go as friends. That left the door open.

"Great. So I'll talk to you at school on Monday?"

"Yeah. Definitely," Tyler said. He watched her walk to her car and get in. Her mom glanced over at Tyler and waved from the open window. Tyler waved back as his face heated up. It seemed like he had a real chance with Julia now, with their first date and Spring Fling coming up. He was ready to give it his best shot. His dad's words echoed again: *You appreciate things more if you have to earn them.*

Then Tyler had a sudden burst of energy and jogged back to where his mom and dad were still talking.

They turned to Tyler as he walked up.

"Okay, let's go."

His parents were smiling knowingly at each other. "What was that about?" His dad's eyes flashed over to where Julia's mom's car was pulling out of the lot.

"Nothing. I'll tell you later," Tyler said, wishing the flush in his cheeks would go away. "Can we go home now? I'm starving."

"Absolutely," said his dad. "You can tell us everything over dinner. Your mom's going to join us, if that's okay."

"Yeah, I mean, sure. That's okay by me," Tyler said, trying to seem nonchalant about it despite the grin taking over his face again.

He slid into the front seat of his dad's car, watching as his mom's SUV pulled up behind theirs to follow them out of the parking lot.

Now Tyler had better things to focus on than his mistake at State or even this disaster of a day. His team had survived a dust storm, his parents were getting along, and he was going to the Spring Fling dance. This was going to be an awesome spring.

DAY OF DISASTER

AFTERSHOCK
BACKFIRE
BLACK BLIZZARD
DEEP FREEZE
VORTEX
WALL OF WATER

Would you survive?

ABOUT THE AUTHOR

Kristin F. Johnson lives in Minneapolis, Minnesota, and teaches writing at a local college. She spent two years as a media specialist and children's librarian in Minneapolis Public Schools. In 2013 and again in 2015, she won Minnesota State Arts Board Artist Initiative grants for her writing. She loves dogs and has a chocolate Labrador retriever.